Master Bun

by ALLAN AHLBERG

with pictures by
FRITZ WEGNER

PUFFIN

PUFFIN BOOKS

Published by the Penguin Group
Penguin Books Ltd, 80 Strand, London WC2R 0RL, England
Penguin Group (USA), Inc., 375 Hudson Street, New York, New York 10014, USA
Penguin Books Australia Ltd, 250 Camberwell Road, Camberwell, Victoria 3124, Australia
Penguin Books Canada Ltd, 10 Alcorn Avenue, Toronto, Ontario, Canada M4V 3B2
Penguin Books India (P) Ltd, 11 Community Centre, Panchsheel Park, New Delhi – 110 017, India
Penguin Group (NZ), cnr Airborne and Rosedale Roads, Albany, Auckland 1310, New Zealand
Penguin Books (South Africa) (Pty) Ltd, 24 Sturdee Avenue, Rosebank 2196, South Africa

Penguin Books Ltd, Registered Offices: 80 Strand. London WC2R 0RL, England

puffinbooks.com

First published by Viking 1988
Published in Puffin Books 1988
29 30

Text copyright © Allan Ahlberg, 1988
Illustrations copyright © Fritz Wegner, 1988

Educational Advisory Editor: Brian Thompson

Manufactured in China
Set in Century Schoolbook by
Filmtype Services Limited, Scarborough

British Library Cataloguing in Publication Data
A CIP record for this book is available from the British Library

ISBN-13: 978-0-14032-344-3

Bertie Bun was born to be a baker.
His dad was a baker.
His mum was a baker.
His grandmas and grandpas were bakers.
His uncle was a boxer –
but that's another story.

When he was a baby, Bertie loved
to play with the flour and water.
When he was a little boy,
he loved to carry the bread.
But when he grew older, things changed.

One morning Bertie Bun
climbed out of bed,
came down for breakfast and said,
"I am browned off with bread –
and bored with baking."
"Oh, don't say that," said Mr Bun.
And Mrs Bun said, "Eat your toast!"

Later, Bertie went out
to deliver the bread.
On the way he met Billy Bone
the butcher's boy.
"I wish I was a butcher's boy,"
said Bertie. "Bread's boring."
"Let's swop, then," said Billy.
So they did.

But this only led to trouble.
Billy got lost with the bread,
and a bad dog ran off
with Bertie's sausages.

The dog belonged to Mr Creep the crook –
but that's another story.

Bertie came home for his lunch.
"I am very browned off with bread," he said.
"That's what you said this morning,"
said Mr Bun.
And Mrs Bun said, "Eat your sandwiches!"

In the afternoon Bertie delivered
the bread he should have delivered
in the morning.

On the way he met Barry Brush
the barber's boy.
"I wish I was a barber's boy,"
said Bertie. "Bread's boring."
"Let's swop then," said Barry.
So they did.
But this only led to more trouble.
Barry fell in the river with the bread,

and Mr Brush gave Bertie a free haircut
that he didn't really want.

Bertie came home for his tea.
"I am as browned off as ever with bread,"
he said.
"You're bald as well," said Mr Bun.
And Mrs Bun said,
"Eat your bread-and-butter pudding!"

Later that evening, Bertie played football, had a bath and went to bed.

In the night he dreamt he was:

a bus-driver's boy

a bandleader's boy

a balloonist's boy

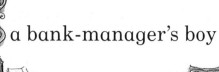
a bank-manager's boy

a bank-*robber*'s boy

a ballet-dancer's boy

and a bishop's boy.

He also had a bad dream
about loaves with little legs –
but that's another story.

The next day Bertie Bun
was still browned off with bread;
and the next day, and the next day,
and the next.
But the *next* day
Billy Bone came to tea.
"These sandwiches are good," he said.
"I wish my mum was a baker –
all I get is sausages."
And Bertie thought about this.

A few days later
Barry Brush came to tea.
"This bread-and-jam is beautiful," he said.
"I wish my dad was a baker –
all I get is haircuts."
And Bertie thought about *this*.

That evening Bertie watched
his mum and dad baking the bread.
He felt the heat from the ovens;
he smelled the hot-bread smell
in the air . . .
and was *not* bored.

The next morning Bertie Bun
climbed out of bed,
came down for breakfast and said,
"Bread's not so bad!"
"Hooray!" said Mr Bun.
"This son of ours is using his loaf."
"More toast, please!" said Bertie.
And Mrs Bun said, "Crumbs!"

Later, Bertie went out
to deliver the bread.
On the way he met Billy Bone
and Barry Brush –

and a performing dog.
The dog belonged to Mr Cosmo
the conjuror.
"I wish I was a conjuror's boy,"
said Bertie.
And Billy said...

... but, no.
What Billy said
and what Barry said
and what Bertie *did*, will have to wait.
There's no more room in the book.
And, besides, it really is . . .

. . . another story.

The End